To my grandfather, who demonstrated patience.—D.J.

Copyright © 1989 Rabbit Ears Productions. Inc., Westport, Connecticut.
Rabbit Ears Books is an imprint of Rabbit Ears Productions.
Published by Picture Book Studio Ltd., Saxonville, Massachusetts.
Distributed in Canada by Vanwell Publishing, St. Catharines, Ont.
Printed in Hong Kong.
10 9 8 7 6 5 4 3 2 1
Library of Congress Cataloging in Publication Data
Andersen, H.C. (Hans Christian), 1805–1875.
Thumbelina / Hans Christian Andersen ; edited by Tom Roberts ;
illustrated by David Johnson.
Summary: A tiny girl no bigger than a thumb is stolen by a great ugly
toad and subsequently has many adventures and makes many animal
friends, before finding the perfect mate in a warm and beautiful
southern land.
ISBN 0-88708-113-4
ISBN 0-88708-114-2 (bk. & cassette package)
[1. Fairy tales.] I. Roberts, Tom, 1944– . II. Johnson, David, 1951–
ill. III. Title. PZ8.A542Th 1989 839.8'136—dc20 [E] 89-8484

written by Hans Christian Andersen
adapted by Tom Roberts

THUMBELINA

illustrated by David Johnson

Rabbit Ears Books

Quite a long time ago there lived in Denmark a couple who worked very hard yet still were quite poor. But more than money, more than anything, they wanted a child.

When that didn't come to be, the wife went to see the witch down the road to ask her for her help. The witch said to her, "I have a present for you. Barley. A special grain of barley. Plant this and we shall see about your wish." The witch smiled and returned to her garden of weeds.

The wife hurried home and planted the grain. While the soil was still on her hands, there sprang up a large, most unusual flower. The wife looked, and looked again. There in the middle of the flower sat a tiny, radiantly beautiful girl, no bigger than the wife's thumb. "I shall call her Elena." And she did. But everyone else called her Thumbelina.

The wife shaped a walnut shell into a cradle for Thumbelina and she plucked a rose petal for a blanket. People came from several towns away to see this remarkable little girl.

One night while Thumbelina slept, a big, slimy old toad hopped through a broken windowpane and landed right next to her.

"Braaaaghx. Here's a prrretty little girl who would be a fine wife for my son." And with that, the old toad lifted the shell cradle and hopped back through the broken windowpane.

At the old toad's dank home, her eyesore of a son, even more grotesque than his mother, stared in wonder at the sleeping Thumbelina.

"She shall make you a fine wife."

"Braaaaghx!" crowed the young toad, his slimy skin glistening in the moonlight.

When morning came, Thumbelina woke and looked around for her mother.

Thumbelina was puzzled. "What has happened to my old home?"

"You shall be my son's brrride and you shall live happily together in the sludge by the pond." She smiled a smile that frightened Thumbelina, and the bubbles doubled round the young toad's eyes.

As the two toads slithered off through the darkly sparkling water, Thumbelina was anything but happy. She sat, all alone and oh so sad in the middle of a leaf in the middle of a pond.

She thought very hard how to escape from a horrible life with a terrible toad.

As she thought, she noticed little fish swimming all around her. She called to them. "Can you help me, little fish?" And the fish, who had never liked the toads, swam down to the stem of the lily pad and gnawed at it till the leaf floated free. Just then, a butterfly fluttered by and lit upon her leaf. Thumbelina untied her sash and tied one end to her leaf and the other to the butterfly. So away she went, out of the pond and into a stream, out of the stream and into a river, passing towns great and small.

Birds would spy her and sing out, "What a pretty girl. What a pretty girl."

All of a sudden, Thumbelina heard a frightful buzzing above her head. She looked up to see a dreadfully big June bug diving down at her. She ducked and swatted at him, but he snatched her up with two of his six spindly legs and carried her off towards a towering tree.

The June bug set her down on a lofty leaf. "You are a dazzzzling thing, though my taste uzzzually runzzz to June bugzzz." As he spoke, some other June bugs landed and began to look her over. Some of the young females, their antennae aquiver, were rather waspish in their comments. "Look at that! Only two legzzz!"

"And so skinny."

"Where are her antennae?"

"Hideous. Simply hideous."

Thumbelina had an idea. "Oh, I am ugly. I am. What shall I do surrounded by such beauty?" The lady June bugs' antennae pulsed with pride. Thumbelina went on. "I don't deserve to dwell amid such splendor."

The male June bug, who had snatched her up because she was so pretty, felt embarrassed. "Let her go where she pleazzzezzz." Nodding to his nitpicking sisters, he dropped Thumbelina from the treetop. Down and down she tumbled, till she spread her skirt so the wind filled it. Then she floated gently towards the ground and landed lightly on a daisy.

For the whole summer, Thumbelina lived happily in the forest, listening to the sweet song of the birds and walking among the thousand flowers that grew there.

Summer passed into fall. The birds headed for their winter homes. The leaves fell from the trees. Thumbelina shivered from the cold and had to walk farther and farther for food.

One day as she searched for food, she found herself at the homestead of a field mouse. Weakly, she knocked at the door and the good-hearted old mouse opened up, saw her and took her in immediately.

It was warm inside. "Please, sir, I am so hungry. May I have some food?"

"Of course, of course," replied the mouse. Off he shuffled into the kitchen and returned with a steaming plate of barley and broth and nuts.

"Oh, thank you, Mr. Mouse," said Thumbelina sweetly.

"Yes, well then. Stay. Stay the winter if you wish," squeaked the mouse.

For the first time in many weeks, Thumbelina was happy.

One day the mouse grew very excited. "My neighbor is coming to visit. Oh, heee is a fine fellow, with a magnificent mansion and a splendid velvet suit. Of course, heee can scarcely seee, but heee is oh so refined. A fine husband heee would make." Thumbelina smiled at the mouse's tender concern, and she was curious about this visitor. But she wasn't interested just yet in finding herself a husband.

The visitor arrived and Thumbelina's heart sank—he was nothing but a mole. His velvet suit was lovely, and he was clearly very refined. But he couldn't bear the light of day and he sneered at everything about the daylight: at flowers and streams, at singing birds and green green grass. "Fffmuh!" he snorted, "Give me a deep, dark room any time."

The mole, although he could not see her, fell in love. But being a prudent mole, he said nothing. He did, however, invite Thumbelina to visit him in his magnificent underground mansion.

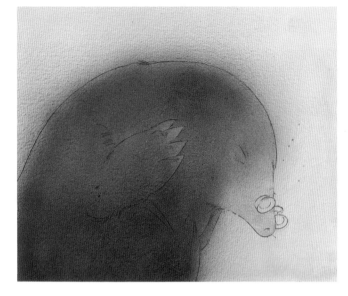

The mole led Thumbelina and the field mouse through the tunnel towards his mansion. As they rounded a bend, the mole announced, "Do not be concerned, my dear, about this infernal bird," and he kicked a poor dead swallow lying there.

"I am glad I am not a bird," snuffed the mole. "All that chirp, chirp, chirping and when winter comes, they are too stupid to stay alive."

Thumbelina remained silent, for she loved birds. As the others pressed on towards the mole's mansion, she lifted the bird's frigid feathers and kissed the poor dead creature on its closed eyes. "Perhaps," she said, "it was you who sang so sweetly for me this summer. Poor dear bird, you made me happy and now you are so cold." She laid her head on the bird's breast, but trembled as she felt a stirring. His heart was beating! The bird was only numb and Thumbelina's warmth had thawed him.

The bird awoke, but was too weak to move. Thumbelina gave him some crumbs she had to help him grow stronger. "A thousand, thousand thanks to you. With your help, I shall soon be well enough to fly again in the warm sunshine."

And so the winter passed with Thumbelina nursing the swallow back to health. And with each day, she and the bird grew fonder of each other. But she never mentioned him to the mouse or the mole.

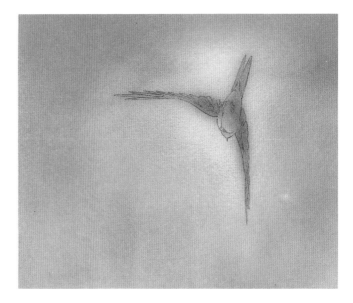

Before too long, spring returned and the earth warmed and the swallow told Thumbelina it was time again for him to fly.

The swallow tried his wings, soaring off in a circle high above the tiny girl. He lit again beside her and asked, "Won't you come away with me and live in the deep green forest?"

"No," she answered, "I cannot. I must stay with the mouse."

"Then farewell. But for you, I would be under the ground, not soaring above it. Though you are small, your heart is great."

With that the swallow took off and flew straight up into the bright sunshine. Far below, Thumbelina watched through her tears as her truest friend grew smaller and smaller and disappeared into the forest.

When she returned home, the field mouse was even more agitated than usual.

"Oh my," squeaked the mouse, "it's happened, it's happened. Mr. Mole has asked for your hand in marriage."

"Well," thought Thumbelina, "he didn't ask me." But to the mouse, all she said was, "Oh?"

"You are like a daughter to meee, my deeear. I have employed four of the best spinners in the fieeeld to work on your trousseau."

Thumbelina smiled at the field mouse's kindness, but her heart sank with double sadness—to be separated from her truest friend, and to be doomed to a life of darkness with the mole.

Every day, she would leave the spinning spiders and go out to breathe in the fragrance of her beloved flowers. And she would gaze up through the blades of grass at the deep blue sky. How she treasured those times, for she knew that with the mole, she would never see the sun, never smell the flowers. And all the while she would scan the sky for the swallow, and listen for his song.

But the swallow did not come.

Every evening, the mole would call on her with great formality. Never did he fail to say how he longed for the summer to end. "When it is gone and the dark days are with us again, you and I will be wed."

And each time he said that, Thumbelina's heart sank deeper.

All too soon, you can be sure, summer came to an end. The scent of flowers grew dimmer and the sky was dark more than it was light.

"Your wedding is just a weeeek away," exclaimed the mouse as he bustled about with the guest list.

Thumbelina could contain herself no longer. She drew herself up to her full two inches and declared, "I will never marry that dreadful, dark-abiding, mean-mouthed, monstrous old mole!"

The mouse dropped his guest list and his jaw.

"I will not," she repeated.

"Rubbish!" shrieked the mouse. "You should beeee grateful. Beeeesides, how could I ever explain? Imagine! Just imagine!" And with that, the mouse turned and walked away.

The wedding would take place, that much was certain.

The day before the wedding, Thumbelina walked sadly through the grass for one final look at the sky. She felt the warmth of the sun on her face and closing her eyes, she thought she could hear the chirping song of the swallow. Thumbelina smiled at the memory.

"I shall never again see you, my truest friend," and in her mind heard again the swallow's song.

"I must not torment myself," she said aloud.

"Then come away with me." It was the swallow.

Thumbelina told her friend of the life she would lead, without sun, without birds, without trees and without flowers, her beloved flowers.

"I am headed towards sunny, peaceful lands where the flowers always bloom," said the swallow. "You must let me carry you there."

Thumbelina needed no convincing. She leapt onto the swallow's back and put her feet onto his outspread wings. Up they went, climbing over trees and then swooping down along golden meadows, across silvery lakes, through shimmering valleys. Thumbelina shivered as they soared over snow-topped mountains, but she snuggled under the swallow's warm downy feathers.

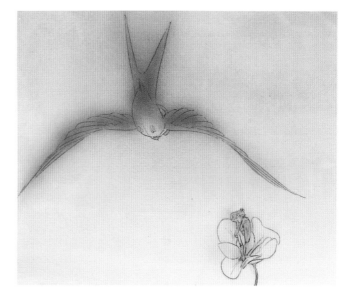

On they went, and soon they were in the sunny countries.

Beneath them Thumbelina saw a magnificent lake. On one side of the lake rose a white marble palace with tall, graceful columns. Atop each column perched a nest. It was to one of these that the swallow headed, Thumbelina on his back.

"What a beautiful home you have here. But it's so high. Is there nowhere below where I might stay?"

"You gave me back my life," answered the bird. "I shall give you the happiness you have earned. Choose any flower and it will be your home."

The swallow gathered her up and swooped down to hover above the flowers. Thumbelina noticed that inside each flower stood a tiny person, no taller than herself.

"But who are they?" she asked.

"They are the flower angels," explained the swallow. "In each flower lives a tiny angel. They are very like you."

Thumbelina was about to speak when she spotted one tiny angel, radiantly handsome and more magnificent than the rest. On his shoulders was a pair of splendid white wings, and on his head was a graceful golden crown.

"The king of the flower angels."

The king stood transfixed at the sight of Thumbelina. "How utterly beguiling," thought the king. "She is the most beautiful girl I have ever seen." And truly she was.

As Thumbelina stepped onto his flower, the king removed his crown and bowed. Thumbelina glowed as she returned the king's gesture.

"How wonderful," she thought. "I wish I might be married to someone as remarkable as this king of my own size."

The king, it should come as no surprise, was having very similar thoughts.

It was not very many days before the king placed his crown on Thumbelina's head. They were married, accompanied by the song of the swallow, who was pleased that at last Thumbelina had found contentment. The flower angels showered her with gifts, but the greatest of these was from the king: a pair of white gossamer wings. And she was very, very happy.

When spring came, the swallow bade farewell and soared off into the north for a few months. There he built his nest over the window of a cobbler's shop and told the cobbler this story. And the cobbler has passed it on to us.